Perfect

This book belongs to

_____

_____

_____

Nicola Davies

Illustrations Cathy Fisher

Perfect
First published by Graffeg May 2016
This edition published April 2017
Copyright © Graffeg 2016
ISBN 9781910862469

Text © Nicola Davies 2016.
Illustrations © Cathy Fisher 2016.
Designed and produced by Graffeg
www.graffeg.com

Graffeg Limited, 24 Stradey Park Business
Centre, Mwrwg Road, Llangennech,
Llanelli, Carmarthenshire SA14 8YP
Wales UK Tel 01554 824000
www.graffeg.com

2 3 4 5 6 7 8 9

Perfect

Nicola Davies

Illustrations Cathy Fisher

GRAFFEG

I loved the little bedroom on the top floor of our pointy house. In summer, swifts nested in the roof above it and I watched their fledglings' first flights from its window. They were perfect from the very start, soaring high to slice the sky with crescent wings.

All winter I waited for them to return. And I waited for the baby who would sleep in the tiny rooftop room.

The day she came was the same day that the swifts came back. They raced and chased each other, screaming over rooftops with the joy of being home.

I watched them from the window. That's how it will be, I thought, me and my sister, racing and chasing, screaming with laughter and delight.

But when my sister came home from the hospital,
I could see that she would never race or chase. She didn't even
scream. Her dark eyes looked at me and she lay quite still.

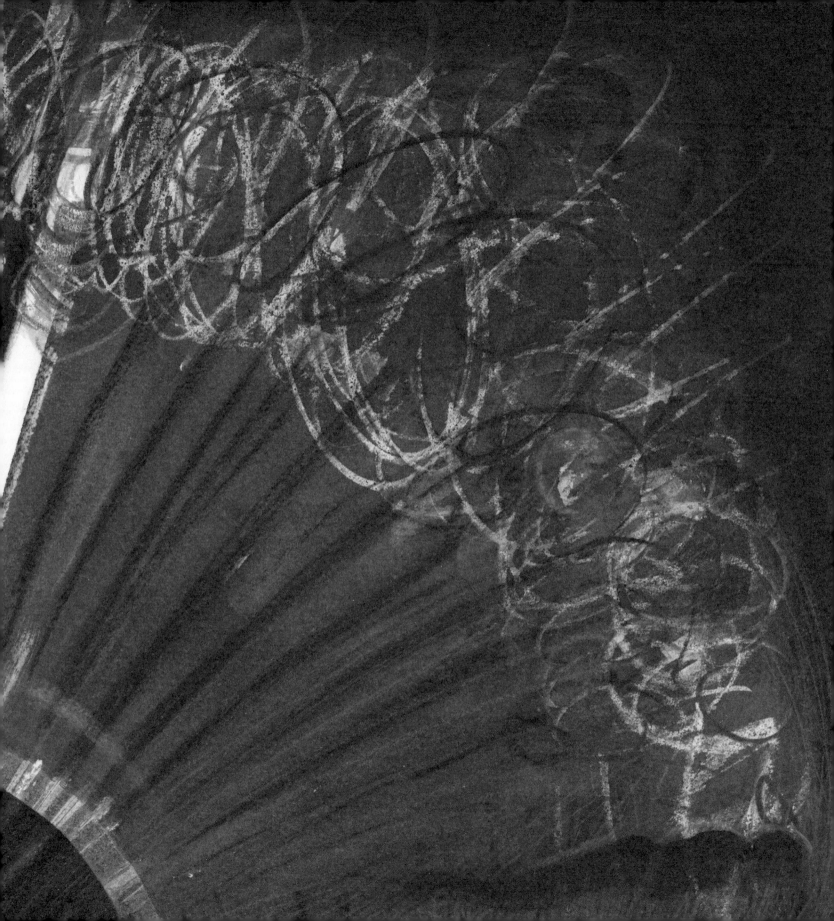

I didn't want to hold her so I ran into the garden. I lay there, on my back, to watch the swifts and let my tears run down into the grass, where nobody would see them.

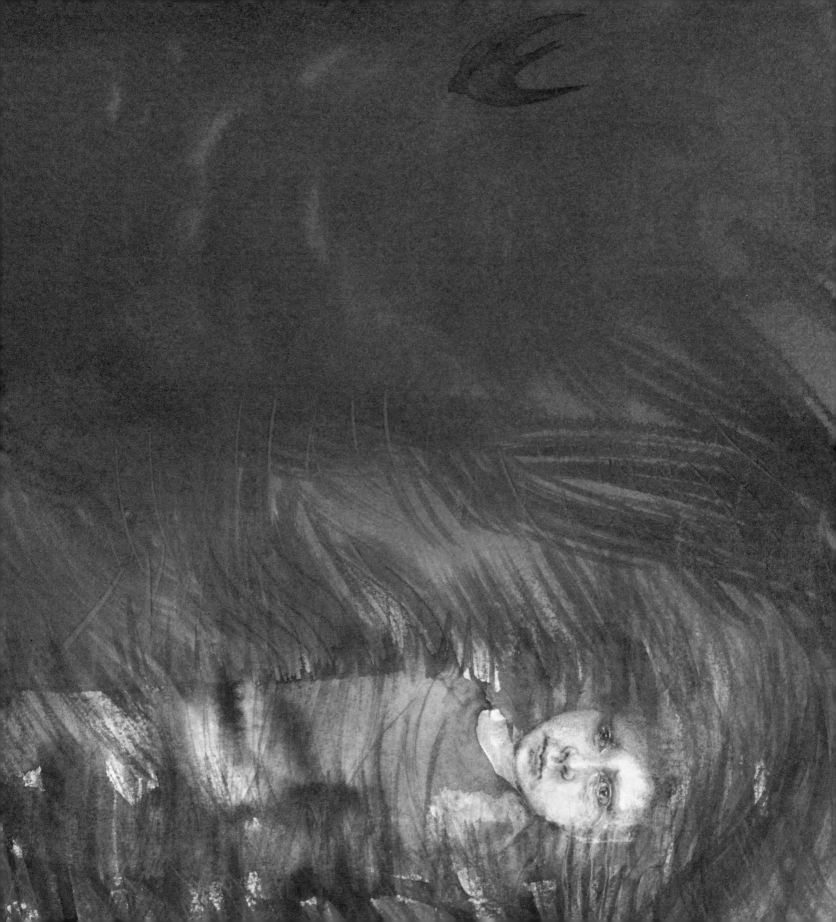

All summer long I played outside, alone.

When people asked about my sister, I turned my head away.

I didn't want to feel the way I felt. But I couldn't love my sister, no matter how I tried.

Every night I watched the swifts fly up and up into the dusk. They disappeared into the blue. Sometimes I wished that I could vanish with them.

Every morning they'd be back, snipping at the air between the rooftops with their scissory wings, their screams as sharp as arrows pointing to the stillness in my sister's room. From outside in the garden, I'd watch them, visiting their nests in the roof above her quiet window.

Then, one August dawn, I saw something on the grass, like a sooty piece of half burned paper from a garden bonfire: a fledgling swift had crashed onto the lawn.

Down on the ground it looked all wrong: its puny legs too small, its crumpled wings too long, but when I gently stretched them out, they were quite perfect. Its dark eye looked at me as it lay quiet in my hands.

Perhaps, I thought, it only needs a little help.

I went inside, and carried it upstairs, right up to the little bedroom on the top floor of our pointy house.

I opened up the window and held the swift out on my hands, so it could see the sky and feel the air.

Its small feet gripped my finger for a moment, and its body trembled.

Then its wings flickered, fast as thinking and it was gone, scissor-slicing through the morning air until it was a black dot, high above the rooftops.

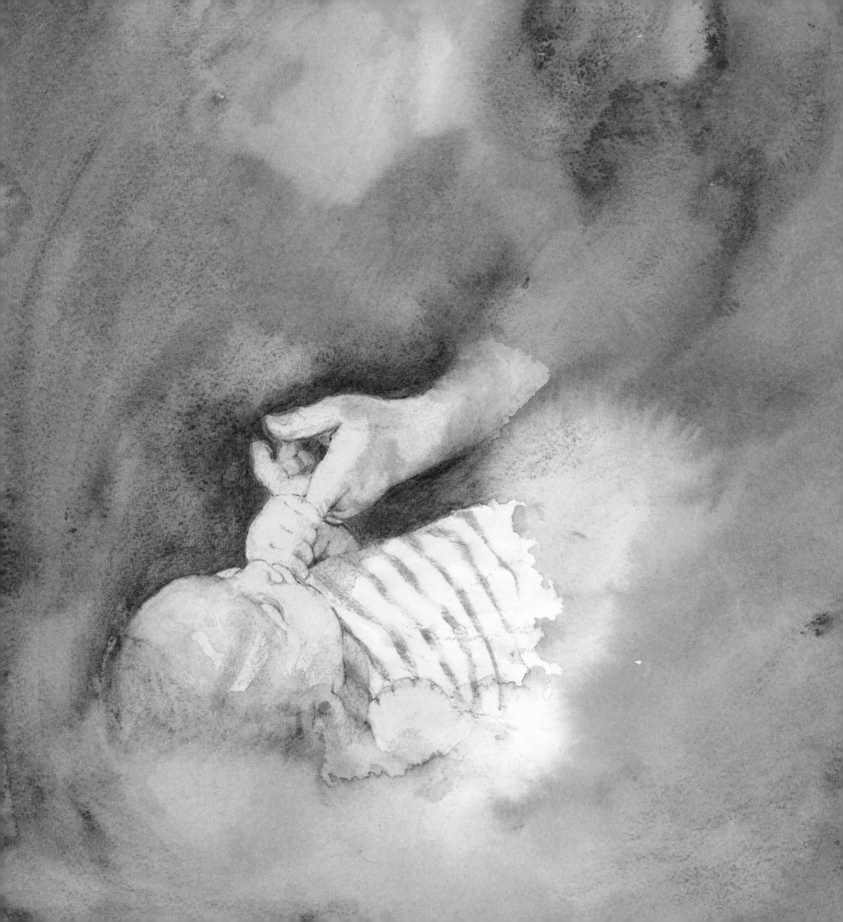

I turned around and stood beside my sister's crib. Her dark eyes opened and her tiny fingers curled tightly onto mine. She smiled at me, a perfect, perfect, perfect smile.

Perhaps, I thought, she only needs a little help.

I picked her up. So small and warm and soft inside my arms. I took her out into the garden and we watched the swifts together.

And I told her how it was going to be, the two of us together, racing,
chasing,
screaming with delight and laughter.

Nicola Davies

Nicola is an award-winning author, whose many books for children include *The Promise* (Green Earth Book Award 2015, Greenaway Shortlist 2015), *Tiny* (AAAS Subaru Prize 2015), *A First Book of Nature*, *Whale Boy* (Blue Peter Award Shortlist 2014), and the Heroes of the Wild Series (Portsmouth Book Prize 2014). She graduated in zoology, studied whales and bats and then worked for the BBC Natural History Unit. Underlying all Nicola's writing is the belief that a relationship with nature is essential to every human being, and that now, more than ever, we need to renew that relationship.

Nicola's children's books from Graffeg include *Perfect*, *The Word Bird*, *Animal Surprises*, *Into the Blue* and the Shadows and Light series: *The White Hare*, *Mother Cary's Butter Knife*, *The Selkie's Mate* and *Elias Martin*.

Cathy Fisher

Cathy Fisher grew up with eight brothers and sisters, playing in the fields overlooking Bath. She has been a teacher and practising artist all her life, living and working in the Seychelles and Australia for many years. Art is Cathy's first language. As a child she scribbled on the walls of her bedroom and ever since has felt a sense of urgency to paint and draw stories and feelings which she believes need to be heard and expressed. *Perfect* was one of these stories.

The Pond by Nicola Davies
Illustrated by Cathy Fisher
ISBN 9781912050703
£11.99

The Pond is a touching picture book about a young boy, and his family, overcoming the loss of his father. This colourful, emotional, powerful book is filled with natural imagery; engaging with the difficult themes of death and loss but also with life, love and the importance of the natural world.